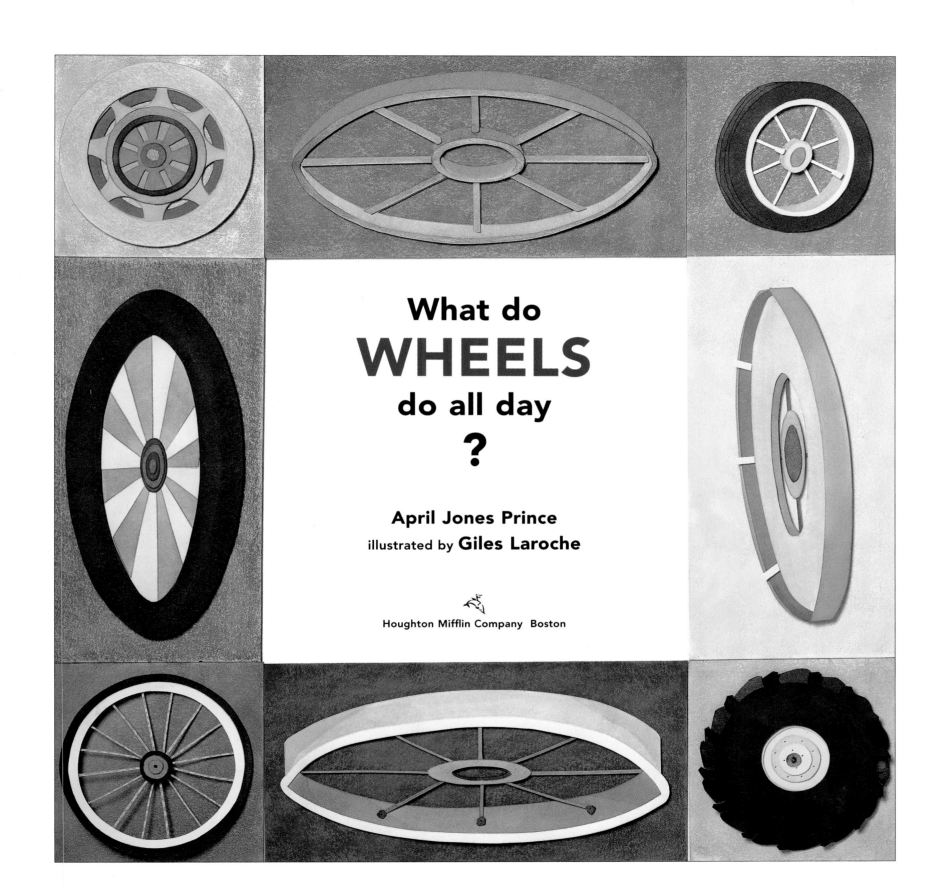

What do
WHEELS
do all day
?

April Jones Prince

illustrated by **Giles Laroche**

Houghton Mifflin Company Boston

With love to Judy Sue,
whose wisdom, warmth, and ideas keep us all rolling.

And in memory of her dear Philemon,
whose vibrant spirit is still whizzing, whirring, and inspiring our work.

—A. J. P.

To my years knowing and working with Philemon and Judy Sue.

—G. L.

Text copyright © 2006 by April Jones Prince
Illustrations copyright © 2006 by Giles Laroche

www.houghtonmifflinbooks.com

The text of this book is set in 50-point Avenir Black.
The paper collage illustrations were created using a combination of drawing, painting, and cutting.

Library of Congress Cataloging-in-Publication Data
Prince, April Jones.
What do wheels do all day? / by April Jones Prince.
p. cm.
ISBN 0-618-56307-5 (hardcover)
1. Wheels—Juvenile literature. I. Title.
TJ181.5.P77 2006   621.8'11—dc22   2004018288

ISBN-13: 978-0618-56307-4

Printed in Singapore
TWP   10   9   8   7   6   5   4
4500268435

What do
WHEELS
do all day
?

Push

Pull

Pedal

Tow

Wheels help

to make us go.

Wheels whiz,

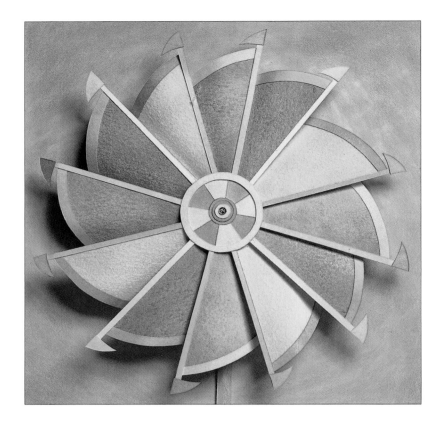

wheels
whir.

Wheels carry

travelers.

Wheels circle,

wheels spin.

Wheels

race . . .

Wheels

win!

Wheels zoom,

wheels putter.

Sometimes wheels

spit and sputter.

Wheels roll,

wheels stroll.

Wheels parade,

and wheels patrol.

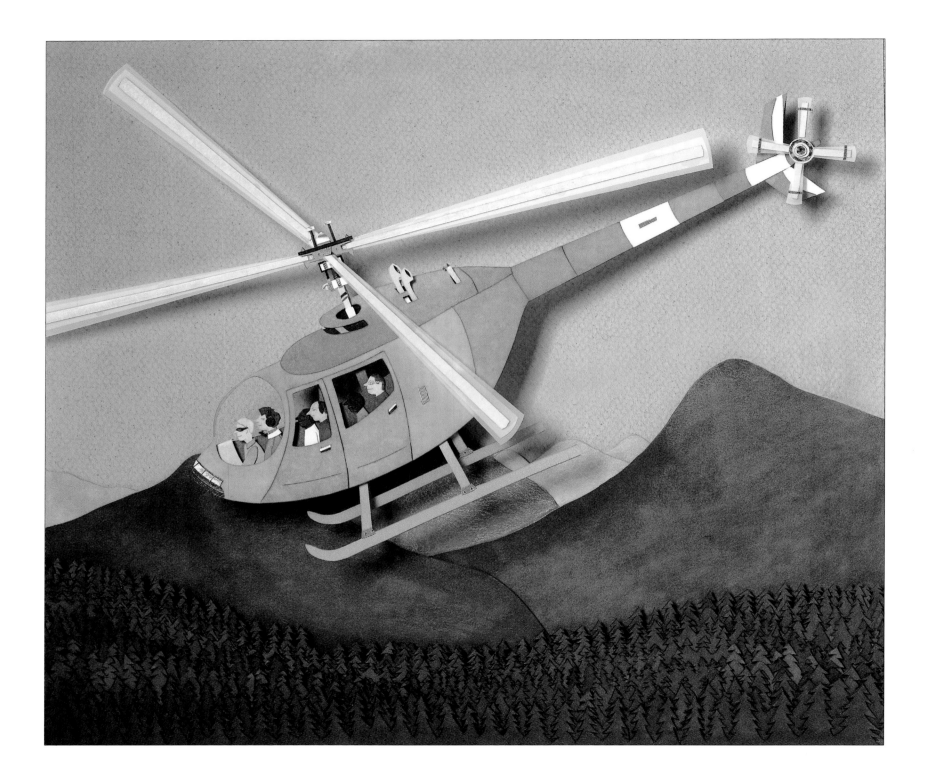

Wheels twirl,

wheels fly.

Wheels soar
into the
sky.

Wheels work,

and wheels play.

That's what
WHEELS
do all day
!